PAIR-IT BOOKS™

Great White SHARKS

Written by Christine Price

STECK-VAUGHN
ELEMENTARY · SECONDARY · ADULT · LIBRARY

A Harcourt Classroom Education Company

www.steck-vaughn.com

How fast can you swim?

Great white sharks can swim a mile in one minute.

How long can you swim?

Great white sharks swim all the time.

Can you swim backward?

Great white sharks can only swim forward.

Do you swim with friends?

Great white sharks swim alone.

Do you swim with your mouth closed?

Great white sharks swim with their mouths open.

Can you swim while you eat?

Great white sharks eat and swim at the same time.

What do you like to eat?

Great white sharks eat fish and meat.

But they cannot eat a cage.